MW01256548

EVERLY DALTON'S DATING DISASTERS

CLAIRE KINGSLEY

Always Have LLC

Copyright © 2019 by Claire Kingsley

All rights reserved.

No part of this book may be reproduced in any form or by any electronic or mechanical means, including information storage and retrieval systems, without written permission from the author, except for the use of brief quotations in a book review.

This is a work of fiction. Any names, characters, places, or incidents are products of the author's imagination and used in a fictitious manner. Any resemblance to actual people, places, or events is purely coincidental or fictionalized.

Published by Always Have, LLC

ISBN: 9781074784072

Edited by Elayne Morgan of Serenity Editing Services

Cover by Lori Jackson

www.clairekingsleybooks.com

❀ Created with Vellum

INTRODUCTION

Everly Dalton is a self-proclaimed dating disaster. Join her as she dishes to her friends on girls' night about her adventures in dating. Will she keep finding frogs, or eventually meet her Prince Charming?

This series originally appeared in Claire Kingsley's newsletter. Each episode chronicles one of Everly's (typically terrible) dates. They take place before the beginning of Everly's book, Faking Ms. Right.

EPISODE 1

EVERLY

"It's official," I said, after the bartender left with our drink orders. "I have the worst dating luck in the history of ever."

It was girls' night, and I'd met my best friends Nora and Hazel for drinks at one of our favorite bars. It was possible we came here a lot. The bartender had even nicknamed us —the *Dirty Martini Running Club*. We did go running— sometimes—but we liked our martinis more.

Nora reached over and squeezed my arm with her perfectly manicured hand. As always, she was the epitome of style in her pretty peach sweater and boyfriend jeans, her thick brown hair cascading around her shoulders. "Aw, honey. That bad?"

"That bad."

"Before you're too hard on yourself, remember luck can't be quantified with data." Hazel adjusted her glasses. Her black and white pintuck dress looked more like work attire than a girls' night dress. But that was Hazel. As was her insistence on using data to prove any assertion.

"We both know it's true," Nora said. "Data or no, Everly is definitely the biggest dating disaster in the history of ever."

I rolled my eyes at her. "Thanks."

"I mean that with love, sweetie," Nora said. "Do you want to tell us, or just drink about it?"

The bartender came back with our martinis, setting them gently on the table.

"I think both." I took a sip. "Okay, so I met Zack on that new dating app."

Nora rolled her eyes. "Well, that was your first mistake."

"I know, I know. But I did all the right things. We texted a little bit before deciding to meet. I swear, there were no red flags. He didn't send dick pics or anything. He seemed so normal."

Hazel and Nora shared a glance.

I took a deep breath. "So we met at Victrola Coffee, and at first, everything was great..."

I WALKED into Victrola Coffee Roasters and smoothed down my shirt. I'd opted for a loose-fitting pink sweater with distressed jeans and ankle boots. Casual, but still cute—and a little sexy. With my blond hair down and wavy, I thought it was a good look for a first date.

Zack was already here, seated at a table near the back. He lifted a hand in greeting and I breathed out a sigh of relief. He actually looked like his profile picture. That was a nice change. The last guy I'd met for coffee had clearly been using a fake photo to hide his male pattern baldness. I hadn't even recognized him.

I smiled and waved back. Zack was cute. Really cute. Thick, dark hair. That dark-brow/blue-eye combination I liked so much. Chiseled jaw. My heart did a little skip as he stood. Tall. So many men lied on their dating profiles about their height. Zack obviously hadn't. His blue shirt and jeans fit his toned frame perfectly.

This guy wasn't just cute. He was hot.

"Hi," I said. "I'm Everly."

"Zack." He walked around to my side of the table and pulled out my chair.

I loved a man with manners. I smiled again as he took his seat across from me, trying not to let too much of my excitement show. This guy was already checking off a lot of boxes. Attractive. Polite. He was a firefighter, and that was just plain hot.

"It's nice to finally meet you in person," I said.

"You too." He took a deep breath and raked his fingers through his thick hair. "Sorry, I'm a little nervous."

Nervous? How about adorable? "Aw, don't be. There's nothing to be nervous about."

The waitress came, and we ordered coffees. He ran his fingers through his hair again. I couldn't possibly be making him nervous, could I? It wasn't like I was Nora. Her aggressiveness made men nervous all the time. She said it weeded out the weak. But I wasn't a self-proclaimed man-eater. I was just a girl looking for my happily ever after.

"So how long have you been a firefighter?" I asked.

"Ten years," he said. "It's been my dream since I was a kid. I think my mom still has pictures of me wearing the plastic hat I got when my preschool class visited the local fire station."

Oh my god, could he be any cuter? "That's so adorable."

"Thanks. What about you? What do you do?"

"I'm an executive assistant," I said, purposefully keeping the details vague. My boss was well-known in Seattle. Dropping his name too soon tended to turn men off.

We engaged in a little more small-talk while we waited for our coffee. It was surprisingly comfortable. By the time the waitress brought our orders, we were both smiling.

"I like your sweater," he said. "That's a nice color."

I plucked at it. "Oh, thank you. One of my best friends helped me pick it out. I usually wear a lot of yellow."

A wave of emotion passed across his face, but it was gone before I could tell what it had been. "Yellow would look good on you."

"Thanks."

He sipped his coffee. "Do you ever wear your hair up?"

I blinked. That was an odd question. "Sure, sometimes. Why?"

"Just wondering."

"Do you have strong opinions about women's hair?"

He shrugged. "I just think it would look good if it was up. Show off your neck and shoulders."

Okay, maybe not so odd. I pulled my hair up and held it, then tilted my chin to the side so he could see.

"Oh yeah," he said, his gaze turning heated. "That's perfect."

Wow. I felt my cheeks flush. His shift from nervous to mildly aggressive was making me a little tingly.

"I guess... maybe next time I'll wear it up."

He fished in his pocket for a second and produced a hair tie. "Maybe you could do it now."

"You want me to put my hair up now?"

He grinned. "Sure. Do you mind?"

I took the hair tie. It was a strange request, but maybe he had a thing for necks and shoulders. I'd let him nibble on my neck a little. Why not?

"Okay. I'll be right back." I went to the bathroom and tried to produce a decent messy bun with no bobby pins or hairspray. And let me tell you, that's not as easy as it sounds.

When I came back, Zack looked me up and down. "Yeah, that's almost perfect."

Almost? "Um, it's kind of hard to do my hair in a public restroom."

"No, no, you look great. Thanks for indulging me." He stood, pulling out his phone. "Can we take a quick selfie?"

"Um." I hesitated, but he flashed me that sexy grin. "Okay."

He put an arm around me and held out his phone. I smiled as he hit the button. We did look awfully cute together. Then he leaned in and planted a kiss on my cheek while he took another. I gasped and caught a glimpse of the picture. My eyes were wide, my lips parted in surprise. Even that one was rather adorable.

"Thanks," he said.

"Sure." I took my seat while he typed something, then set his phone down.

Had he sent the selfie of us to someone? I wasn't sure what was going on. No matter how sexy Zack was, this was taking a turn for the weird.

"Did you send that to someone?"

"Oh, um..." He chewed his lower lip, that endearing nervousness making a reappearance. "Yeah, I kind of did. You look so pretty, I was showing you off."

I touched the stray hairs on the back of my neck, feeling flushed again. Showing me off? "Oh, that's... sweet."

"You're sweet." He pushed his coffee away. "Look, I'm new to dating again, so I'm sorry if I'm doing things wrong."

"Not at all. You're fine."

"Thanks. So... should we go to my place? Or yours?"

My spine straightened. "What?"

"I just moved into a new apartment. It's in walking distance. But if your place would be more comfortable, that's fine too."

Had I just entered an alternate reality, or had my adorably nervous, very hot firefighter just asked me back to his place to hook up?

"Um, that's... a little sudden. I thought we'd have coffee, then make dinner plans or something."

"Oh," he said, leaning back in his chair. "Sorry, I thought coffee was just a warm-up."

I was admittedly attracted to him, and I wasn't judgy about first-date sex. But I wasn't looking for a guy who was just a hook-up, either.

What would Nora do? That was obvious. She'd take him back to her place and enjoy the hell out of that insane body of his. But that wasn't really my style. What about Hazel? She was no help either. She usually ended up arguing with her dates about the scientific method.

"This is just... a little faster than I was thinking," I said. "I thought we were both looking for... a little more."

"Of course I am," he said, flashing me that grin. "I'm sorry, I'm really out of practice. I just feel like the chemistry between us is off the charts. Are you feeling that too, or is it just me?"

I was feeling... something. "I—"

"Oh my god, Zack, are you kidding me with this?"

I looked over to find a woman standing next to our table. She wore a fluttery yellow shirt with jeans and open toed heels. Her hands were on her hips, her blond hair in an expertly done messy bun. She looked a lot like...

That was weird. She looked like me.

"Danielle, what are you doing here?" Zack asked.

Danielle rolled her eyes, her hands still on her hips. "You texted me. Again."

"Did I? I must have hit the wrong button. You didn't have to come all the way over here."

"Are you for real? You know I work next door. And I don't believe for a second you sent me that text by accident."

I cleared my throat, feeling enormously uncomfortable. Was this his ex? He'd picked this café, and she worked right next door? Had he sent her the selfie? Oh god.

"Look, I'm trying to have a nice coffee date with my girl-friend. I don't appreciate the interruption."

Did he just say 'girlfriend'? "Um—"

Danielle snorted. "Right, I'm sure you two have had time to get very serious since I dumped you three weeks ago."

My eyes widened.

"I'm moving on, Danielle. You should think about doing the same."

"Moving on? She looks just like me."

He stood and offered me his hand. "Sorry about this, Everly. Let's just go back to my place."

"Zack, you can bang every blond chick in Seattle for all I care. But stop texting me pictures of you with women who look like me. It's fucking creepy."

I stared at his outstretched hand for a second, then gath-ered up my handbag. "Um, I think I should let you two deal with... whatever it is you're dealing with."

"Everly, don't," he said. "She's crazy, she doesn't know what she's talking about."

"Oh, I'm the crazy one?" Danielle asked. "I'm not the one

who keeps trying to hook up with his ex's lookalikes and sending her pictures as evidence."

I stood so abruptly, I slammed my knee against the table. Both coffees spilled, sloshing hot liquid all over. "Ouch!"

"It figures you'd think this is about you," Zack said.

"You texted me a selfie with her!"

I rubbed my knee, looking back and forth between the two of them. I needed to get out of here. "I'm just going to..."

Neither of them seemed to notice me. As quickly as I could, I dug a five out of my wallet and tossed it on the table to cover my coffee. They were still arguing—something about whether I looked enough like Danielle to qualify as her doppelganger.

Leaving the bickering couple behind, I limped out the door...

"HE PICKED you because you looked like his ex?" Nora asked, her eyebrows lifted.

I nodded. "Yep."

"People generally have physical characteristics they prefer," Hazel said with a slight shrug.

"Having a type is not the same as trying to hook up with ex-lookalikes," Nora said. "And he sent her the selfie? Everly, if I didn't know you, I'd wonder if you made that up."

"Unfortunately, no." My shoulders slumped. "Why am I cursed? I must have done something terrible in a past life. Although I don't know if I believe in past lives."

"It's just a run of bad luck," Nora said. "I'm positive it's going to turn around for you soon."

I sighed, running the tip of my finger along the rim of

my martini glass. "I hope so. How many frogs does a girl have to kiss before she finally finds her prince?"

Nora took a sip of her drink. "Well, there's half your problem right there. You still believe in fairy tales."

She was right. I did believe in fairy tales. I couldn't help it if I was an optimist, especially when it came to love.

He was out there. I was sure of it.

EPISODE 2

EVERLY

*M*y cheeks were still warm from our run as I took a sip of my martini. Yes, we were in a bar right after going for a run. But it was Brody's, a casual place on Phinney, and we liked stopping here after a good workout.

Besides, what better way to reward ourselves for putting in the miles than a martini?

Nora fluffed her still-nice ponytail. I didn't understand how she could look so good after a workout, but she always did. "How was your date the other night, Hazel?"

Hazel pushed her glasses up her nose. She had her gray hoodie zipped and her hair in a braid. "It was fine."

I waited for a few seconds to see if she'd elaborate, but she didn't. "Fine? That doesn't sound very good. I thought you liked this guy."

"I'm hearing a distinct lack of orgasms," Nora said. "I suspect that's the reason for her *fine*."

"Nora is correct," Hazel said. "We don't appear to be physically compatible."

I drizzled a little strawberry vinaigrette over my spinach

salad. "But if you like him enough, maybe you can figure out the physical stuff."

Nora arched an eyebrow at me.

"What?"

"There's some truth to that," Hazel said. "But the non-compatibility extends beyond sexual considerations."

"He's boring," Nora said.

Hazel nodded. "Precisely."

"What about you, Everly?" Nora asked. "You had a date last night. How'd it go?"

"Was it the man who works in your building?" Hazel asked.

"Yep, the hottie in the suit she kept seeing in the lobby," Nora said.

I let out a long sigh.

"Uh-oh." Nora set her martini on the table. "What happened? Spill it, sister."

I took another drink, hoping for some fortification from the crisp bite of gin and vermouth. "Well, he took me to El Gaucho, and I've always wanted to eat there..."

STEPHEN'S HAND brushed the small of my back as we walked to our table. I'd been excited when he'd said he had reservations at El Gaucho. It was fancy for a first date, but I'd always wanted to try it. I'd made reservations before, but for my boss, not for myself. Dinner here was on my wish list.

My date was dressed in a charcoal suit that fit his toned body perfectly. Dark blond hair, neatly trimmed and slicked back. Smooth jaw. It was a good look on him.

His cologne, however, was a bit strong. It didn't smell cheap. Quite the contrary, it had the masculine depth of something designer and expensive. But it lacked the subtlety that made good cologne effective. He'd gone a little overboard, and it tickled my nose every time I got close to him.

We took our seats and I crossed my ankles. I'd chosen a little black dress with a scoop neck and enough fabric that I felt pretty, but not too exposed. My blond hair was up and I was wearing the adorable burgundy heels I'd splurged on recently.

"You look beautiful tonight," Stephen said, his mouth hooking in a slight smile.

"Thank you. And thanks for... this." I gestured to our opulent surroundings. Dark wood and plush leather. Glittering candlelight. A piano played jazz in the background. The whole place felt very retro-glamorous.

"Sure," he said, his eyes darting around for half a second, like he was only minimally impressed.

I picked up the menu and scanned through the selections. El Gaucho was upscale—and pricey. I knew that, but now that it was time to decide what to order, I was a little nervous. What was he going to choose? Maybe I'd insist he go first so I could get a better feel for what he expected.

The server came over—a nice-looking man in his thirties with spiky hair and the sleeves on his black shirt rolled up.

"Good evening," he said. "Can I start you off with a drink? Wine, perhaps?"

Stephen's eyes trailed over the wine list and he rubbed his chin. "We'll have a bottle of Salishan Cellars Reserve Cabernet."

"Excellent choice," the server said. "I'll give you some time to decide on dinner."

I caught a glimpse of the wine list as the server took it.

Had he really just ordered a two-hundred-dollar bottle of wine?

Stephen glanced at his menu briefly, then put it down, as if he'd already decided. He watched me, his eyes panning up and down, and the corner of his mouth lifted again. The way he openly appraised me with that heated gaze made my core tingle.

I tried to keep my attention on the menu, but he bit his bottom lip. God, the bottom lip bite. My body instantly reacted—heart beating faster, cheeks flushing. A rush of heat hit me between the legs, so startling I shifted in my seat.

Wow. I was having a serious physical reaction to this guy.

But I was still wondering about the wine. And how he'd insisted on picking me up, rather than meeting here. The way he'd paused outside his car before opening the door had made me wonder if he was making sure I noticed he drove a Tesla.

The server came back with the wine. He poured a small amount in one glass for us to sample, but before he could pour the second, Stephen held up a finger to stop him. He took the glass, lifted it to his nose, and sniffed. Then he swirled the wine a few times and took a tiny sip.

He set the glass down. "Acceptable. Go ahead."

The only reaction from the server was a slight pinching of his lips. He finished pouring Stephen's wine, then poured mine.

"Thank you so much," I said, flashing the server a bright smile.

It was odd that Stephen hadn't let the server pour a sample for me first. Although I supposed he was paying for it. At least I hoped he was, if this really was two hundred dollars.

I picked up my glass and took a sip. It certainly tasted like two-hundred-dollar wine—or what I imagined two-hundred-dollar wine would taste like. It slipped past my tongue and down my throat like silk. The flavor was rich with a spicy note at the end that lingered on my palate. I'd had nice wines before, but this was incredible.

"Wow," I said, setting my glass down. "No wonder you chose this one. It's delicious."

He took another sip, then peered at his glass as if he were studying the contents. "It's not bad."

"Are you a wine aficionado?"

"I know enough to make sure I always get good quality."

"Ah." Unsure of what else to say, I went back to the menu. "It's hard to decide. What are you thinking?"

"I always get the steak trio."

He made it sound like this was his regular hang-out—like Brody's for me and my girlfriends—not one of the nicer restaurants in Seattle. And the steak trio was one of the most expensive entrees on the menu.

"That does look good," I said. "But it's probably too much food for me."

"Order anything you want," he said with that subtle grin. There was something in his tone that made my back twitch.

Talk about mixed signals. I didn't know what to do with this guy. He looked at me like he wanted me for dessert, and I liked the hints of aggression he was giving me. Like he'd be commanding and bossy—in all the best ways. But I couldn't get over the sense that he was showing off. There was a thin line between confidence and arrogance, and he was leaning to the wrong side.

The server came back and asked to take our orders. Although he looked at me, Stephen piped up first, ordering the Dungeness crab cocktail with prawns, a bowl of truffle soup, and the steak trio.

When he finished, his eyes rested on me, although he was still talking to the server. "And whatever my lovely date wants."

There was that tone again. It wasn't gracious. He didn't sound pleased because he was treating me to a nice dinner. He was smug, like he wanted both me and the server to know this was nothing to him.

Well, then. If he wanted to show off, perhaps I'd let him.

"I'll take the sea scallops to start. Then the delicata squash salad. And the filet medallions." My dinner alone would be over a hundred dollars.

"Excellent," the server said.

After the server left with our orders, I sipped my wine while Stephen launched into a story about his latest vacation—private surfing lessons in Costa Rica. No wonder he was so tan. At first, picturing him wet in nothing but board shorts was a nice image. But he had to emphasize the fact that he'd hired one of the best—and most expensive— surfing instructors in the world.

The appetizers came, and the scallops were melt-in-my-mouth amazing. I had more wine, then started in on my salad while Stephen talked about work, and some of his other exotic vacations. He asked a few questions about me, so at least there was a little give and take. I found myself bouncing back and forth between being interested and feeling that tickle of annoyance at his arrogance.

But it was a first date, and maybe he was just trying to make a good impression.

The server brought our entrees. I was already full from my appetizer and salad, and feeling a little silly for having ordered so much food.

Stephen dug right into his meal. I took my knife and fork and cut a small bite.

"Greece is really amazing, though," he said, picking up the thread of conversation from before our entrees arrived. "There's a villa overlooking the Mediterranean that's one of the most beautiful places I've ever been."

"Sounds lovely." I took another bite.

He grinned again. "I'm planning another trip there in a few months. Maybe I won't have to go alone this time."

I started to swallow so I could reply, when my throat suddenly tightened. My chest contracted painfully and I covered my mouth to keep from coughing.

It was then I realized I couldn't breathe.

I clutched my throat, my eyes widening. Oh my god, I was choking on a piece of steak.

"Everly?" Stephen asked. "Are you all right?"

With my hand still on my throat, I shook my head. I got a thin wisp of air in and out of my lungs—my airway wasn't completely closed off—but my chest burned and panic started to rise.

"Are you going to be sick?" Stephen asked, leaning away from the table.

I shook my head again, faster, and pointed to my throat.

"What are you doing?" he asked, his expression marred by disgust. He glanced around. "Can you just... go to the bathroom until you feel better?"

I took another gasping breath and tried to cough, but the steak wouldn't budge. Why wasn't he helping me?

Stephen adjusted his cuffs and glanced around at the other diners again. "Everly, this is a little much. You're going to cause a scene."

I let out a little squeak—it was all I could get out—and the people at the table next to us looked over.

"Miss, are you okay?"

"Jesus," Stephen said, putting his napkin on the table. "I can't believe you're going to just sit here and vomit on the table."

I shook my head yet again, pointing to my throat. *I'm not going to puke, you asshole; I'm choking!*

"Miss?"

Turning toward the voice, I gestured to my throat again.

"Oh my god, she's choking."

Stephen stood. Finally.

A plump woman wearing a shiny blazer and chunky jewelry darted to my side and hauled me out of my chair. Her arms went around my ribs and she clasped her hands against the base of my sternum. I grunted as she rammed her fists into the base of my chest. Once. Twice. Again.

The piece of steak dislodged and flew out of my mouth. It bounced off the center of our table and rolled onto the floor.

Clutching my hands to my chest, I sucked in a deep breath. In, out. Precious oxygen filled my burning lungs.

"Oh sweetie, are you all right?" The woman stroked my back, like a mother comforting a sick child.

I sank into my chair, wishing I could crawl under the table. All eyes in the restaurant were on me, and some of the wait staff had gathered around our table.

"I think so." My voice came out raspy.

"Here." She handed me a cloth napkin from the table—maybe it had been mine—and pulled Stephen's chair around so she could sit. "Take your time."

"Thank you so much. I was choking, and… I don't know how that happened."

"I'm just glad I was here to help." She nodded toward the empty side of the table. "Especially since your date didn't."

"Wait, where is he?"

"I think he left."

I covered my mouth as I coughed again. "He left?"

She was right. I looked around the restaurant and didn't see any sign of Stephen. He was gone.

"I HAVE SO many problems with this, I don't even know where to begin," Nora said. "Someone had to do the Heimlich maneuver on you last night and we're just now hearing about it?"

I waved her off. "Once it was over, I was fine. My chest is a little sore, but I'm okay."

"You should have called me," Nora said.

"I told you, I'm fine." I took another sip of my martini. "By the time I got home, I just wanted to go to bed."

"You should consider following up with your physician," Hazel said.

"Stephen left?" Nora asked. "You were choking and he left?"

"Yep. Walked right out."

"What an asshole," Nora said.

Hazel nodded. "*Asshole* is a mild word for that kind of deplorable behavior."

"Wait." Nora pointed a manicured finger at me. "Did he stick you with the bill?"

My shoulders slumped. "Yeah, he did."

"You have got to be kidding me," Nora said.

"I couldn't make this stuff up," I said. "You know what? I'm done with men for a while. Maybe forever. What kind of jerk walks away from someone choking?"

"To be fair, Stephen's actions don't represent all men," Hazel said.

"I know, but I thought I was getting something right this time. He seemed so confident and put together. I wouldn't mind a guy who's a bit... commanding, you know? Not controlling or assholeish, but a guy who knows what he wants? That sounded nice. But he bailed when I needed help."

"It's so tempting to camp out in the lobby of your building so I can tell that prick what I think," Nora said.

"Oh my god, please don't," I said. "It's bad enough that he works there. How am I going to avoid him?"

"You're not," Nora said. "You're going to glare at him like he kicked a puppy in front of you and you'll never forgive him for it."

"That's acceptable advice," Hazel said, adjusting her glasses again.

"Thanks, Hazel," Nora said with a smile. Her eyes flicked past me. "Don't turn, but someone's coming to our table."

"What?" I twisted around to look. She was right. A guy dressed in a light gray sweater and slacks was approaching.

"I told you not to look."

"You can't just say *don't look* and expect the person not to."

Nora put her drink down and smiled at the man, flashing her perfect teeth. He was attractive—almost pretty —with stylish blond hair and blue eyes.

"Excuse me ladies," he said with a smile. "I'm sorry to bother you."

"You're not a bother," Nora said.

He turned to me. "This is probably going to sound silly, but my friend over there thinks you're very pretty, but he's too shy to come over and introduce himself."

I glanced over to where his friend stood by the bar. He shook his head and looked away. It was... rather cute. Endearing.

"Well, that's... sweet," Nora said.

"I'm Jake, and my friend is Preston. I tried to get him to come over and say hello, but like I said, he's shy. Would you be willing to write down your number? Maybe I'll be able to talk him into texting you."

I peeked at Preston again. It was hard to tell from this distance, but was he blushing? He was tall and lean, dressed similarly to Jake, in a sweater and slacks. Attractive. Nice hair.

I looked between Hazel and Nora, lifting my eyebrows. *Should I?*

Hazel gave me a little nod. Nora nonchalantly shrugged her shoulders, but that was as good as a yes from her.

"All right," I said. "My name's Everly."

"Thank you, Everly." Jake put a business card on the table, back side up, and handed me a pen. I jotted down my name and number.

"There you go." I pushed the card back toward him.

"Thanks again," Jake said. "You'll be hearing from Preston, if I have anything to say about it."

Jake left and I turned back to my friends.

"Did that just happen?"

"Done with men forever?" Nora asked. "Or just for a day or two until the shy cutie calls?"

I sighed. "I was thinking shy might be a good sign. Stephen was assertive and almost too confident. Even if he hadn't left me while I was choking, it felt like he was showing off all night. Shy could mean sweet. I could do worse than a sweet guy."

Nora shrugged one shoulder. "True, I suppose."

"If you didn't think I should give him my number, why didn't you say so?"

"No, I think it's fine," she said. "He doesn't do it for me, but he wasn't asking for my number anyway. I bet you're right. Shy Preston might be a sweetheart. Who knows, maybe he'll romance the hell out of you."

"That wouldn't be terrible," I said.

My phone buzzed, so I took it out of my purse to look. There was a text from a number I didn't recognize.

Hi, this is Preston. Sorry about Jake.

I glanced up, but Preston and Jake weren't by the bar anymore. Maybe they'd been on their way out when Jake came to our table.

Me: *Nice to meet you. And it's fine.*

Preston: *So... I'm not very good at this, but maybe you'd like to go out sometime?*

"Is it him?" Nora asked.

I nodded as I typed.

Me: *Sure, that would be great.*

Preston: *I'm busy tomorrow—work thing. How about Friday?*

"Well, there you have it," I said, putting my phone away after we'd agreed on the details. "I have a date with Preston."

"Good for you, sweetie," Nora said.

I smiled. A shy, sweet guy. Maybe that was just what I needed.

EPISODE 3
EVERLY

I nestled into the softness of my bean bag chair—it's super comfortable, don't judge—with a glass of chardonnay in hand. Hazel and Nora settled onto the couch, one in each corner. Hazel pulled a yellow throw blanket over her pajama-clad lap, while Nora picked a piece of fuzz off her leggings.

The facial masks we wore made us all look a bit like we were getting ready for a costume party and dressing as geishas. But Nora had assured us our skin was going to glow.

Slumber party? Not quite. Girls' night in? Definitely.

"How do you make that so cute?" Nora asked, pointing at me with a red-manicured finger.

I glanced down at my favorite faded t-shirt. It said *You See A Glass Half-Empty, I See Room For Vodka* with a cute little cocktail glass. I'd paired it with flannel pants that didn't come close to matching and a pair of yellow slippers.

"Are you making fun of my comfy clothes? It's girls' night in. That's low, Nora."

"I'm not, I swear. I mean it, you're so adorable even that hideous color combination is cute on you."

"Oh. Thanks."

Hazel poked an index finger against her cheek. "This is starting to tingle. I'm not certain it's functioning properly."

"No, the tingling is normal," Nora said. "That means it's working."

"Where's the package?" Hazel asked. "I want to check the list of ingredients."

Nora waved a hand. "They're all-natural and organic."

"Neither *organic* nor *all-natural* necessarily equates to *safe*," Hazel said.

"Hazel, it's not like Nora would give us something that was bad for our skin," I said. "You know how seriously she takes her beauty regimen."

"That's true," Hazel said.

"I'm telling you, these are fabulous." Nora turned her gaze back on me. "Okay, enough chit-chat. How did things go with Preston?"

"Right." I let out a sigh. "About that..."

"He was a jerk in disguise, wasn't he?" Nora asked.

"Oh, no, Preston was very nice," I said. "But I'm not seeing him again."

"Why not?"

"Well..."

❦

PRESTON SAT ACROSS FROM ME, dressed in a crisp button-down shirt and slacks. His blond hair was neatly trimmed, his face smooth. He was attractive and well-groomed. Polite, soft-spoken. A good listener. His friend had called him shy, but now that we were chatting, he seemed relaxed. A little reserved, maybe, but we'd been having a good time.

The problem? He wasn't doing a thing for me in the attraction department.

As we chatted, I tried to figure out what was wrong with this picture. My last date had been an absolute jerk, yet I'd been undeniably attracted to him. Until he'd left me while I was choking on a piece of steak and stuck me with the bill, that is. I'd never date a man like Stephen—not more than once, anyway—but there had been something appealing about his confidence. His assertiveness.

Preston was just as physically attractive as Stephen had been. Perhaps more so, depending on one's particular tastes. Tall, lean. Well-dressed. He smelled nice.

So why did I feel absolutely nothing in any place that counted?

It wasn't that I was looking to jump in bed with him. But was some good old-fashioned physical attraction too much to hope for?

He lifted his mug and sipped the last of his coffee. Mine was already empty. I figured he was about to tell me it was nice to meet me and that would be that.

"This has been nice," he said. His brow creased slightly, as if that was an unexpected revelation.

"It has been." And I meant that. It had been nice. But was 'nice' enough for a second date?

"I think I'm all coffeed out, but..." He hesitated, like he was making a decision. "I need to run over to the mall. Shopping isn't really my thing, so I've been avoiding it. But maybe it would be fun to go together. Care to join me?"

Okay, so I didn't exactly want to drop my panties for him, but we'd had a good time so far. And I did like him. A little shopping would probably be fun.

And maybe I could figure out why I wasn't feeling any fun little flutters of excitement when I looked at him.

"Sure, I'd love to."

"Great."

The air outside was crisp, but not too cold. I was dressed in my favorite pale blue trench coat, jeans, and a cute pair of flats. I'd driven myself, so I walked to my car and got in. The mall wasn't far. I followed Preston and parked next to him.

Just as we got inside, my phone binged with a text.

"Do you mind if I check this?"

Preston paused next to me. "Not at all."

I pulled my phone out of my purse. It was Nora.

Nora: *Obligatory serial killer check*

Me: *Excuse me?*

Nora: *Shy guy? Serial killer? It was hard to tell at the bar. Are you alive?*

Me: I'm texting you back, aren't I?

Nora: Someone is. We need proof of life.

Me: We?

Nora: *I'm at Hazel's.*

I held up my phone and snapped a quick selfie.

Me: *See? I'm fine.*

Nora: *Good girl. Carry on.*

"Everything all right?" Preston asked.

"It's just my girlfriends checking on me." I tucked my phone back in my purse.

"Good friends," he said.

"They really are."

We wandered through the mall, side-by-side. Preston didn't seem to be in any hurry, but he kept his hands to himself. No hand on my back or light touch on my elbow. The closest he'd come to touching me was when he'd helped me out of my coat at the coffee shop. Maybe that was his shyness coming through. He was very reserved.

The sweet smell of cinnamon rolls filled the air and I

slowed to enjoy it. Preston glanced at me with a little half-smile on his face.

"Want one?"

"A cinnamon roll?" Did I ever. But I wasn't about to eat a sticky mass of sugary carbs when I was on a first date.

"Yeah." He raised his eyebrows. "I'll share one with you."

That was so very tempting. And the way Preston grinned at me, like a kid about to sneak a cookie from his grandma's cookie jar, made it all the more enticing.

"Come on," he said. "When was the last time you had trashy mall food?"

"I don't even know."

"Me neither. I won't tell anyone if you don't."

I laughed. "Okay, you twisted my arm."

He bought a cinnamon roll and drizzled frosting over the top. We alternated tearing off bites as we walked.

"So is this a typical date strategy?" I asked. "Meet a girl for coffee, then fill her up with baked goods?"

He chuckled. "No, not really. It's fun, though, right?"

"It is."

I gazed at him for a second. He was undeniably hand-some. But still doing nothing for me.

After we finished the decadent cinnamon roll, we went into a department store and headed for the men's section.

"Are you looking for something in particular?" I asked.

"My office recently instituted casual Fridays, and I have a remarkable lack of casual-Friday clothing options."

"Let me guess. To you, casual just means no tie?"

He smiled. "Basically, yes."

"Okay, let's see what we can find."

I led him straight to men's casual wear and started looking through the racks. A less-buttoned-up Preston might be rather sexy. Maybe he just needed to loosen up a little bit. I'd liked his grin when he'd suggested we eat naughty food. Was there a sex god lurking behind that straight spine and what looked like manicured hands?

He paused to glance at a rack of shirts, and I took a moment to look him up and down. I tried to imagine him a little messy. Hair tousled, a few days without shaving. Would that do it for me?

I still wasn't seeing it.

Why didn't I feel anything for him? He was attractive, put-together, well-dressed. But there was zero chemistry. No spark at all.

Oh my god, maybe the problem was me.

I'd been attracted to Stephen, and he'd turned out to be a huge asshole. Now here was Preston—the epitome of a nice guy—and he wasn't doing anything for me. Was I one of those women who said she wanted a nice guy, but really wanted a bad boy? Was I doomed to keep dating jerks because they made me tingly between the legs?

We paused again and I ran my fingers over the soft fabric of a shirt. Was I really only attracted to assholes? That couldn't be true. I liked nice guys, even shy ones. I'd taken a chance on Preston, even though he'd been too timid to talk to me himself.

A man in a short-sleeved shirt and well-fitting jeans walked by. My eyes were drawn to the way those jeans hugged his ass. I looked away quickly—I wasn't about to stand here staring at some guy's butt while I was on a date—and noticed Preston looking in the same direction.

Wait...

He tilted his head as the guy walked away, then went back to browsing through the rack of clothes.

Had I just imagined that? Or had we both been checking out the same guy?

"This is nice," I said, holding up a dark blue shirt.

Preston slid the sleeve between his thumb and forefinger. "It's not bad."

Another man walked by as I put it back on the rack. Preston's eyes strayed to him.

"He makes those pants look good," I said.

"Yeah," Preston said, almost under his breath, then cleared his throat.

"Were you checking him out?"

"What? No."

I crossed my arms. "Are you sure?"

He sighed out a breath, his shoulders slumping a little. "All right. Maybe. Yes."

"Okay, so..."

"I'm sorry, Everly. I haven't been completely honest with you."

"I'm listening."

He took another deep breath. "I'm gay."

A sudden sense of relief washed over me. He was gay? No wonder there wasn't any chemistry between us. It wasn't because he was a nice guy. It was because we were batting for the same team.

But why was he out on a date with me?

"I'm confused. If you're gay, why did you ask me out?"

"It's a long story."

I raised my eyebrows.

"Okay. I got out of a relationship about six months ago. It was... toxic, to say the least. Jake's been a good friend—he's been there for me—but he came up with this idea."

"What idea? To ask me out?"

He tipped his head. "To go out with a woman. I've known I was gay for a long time, so I've never even been on a date with a woman. Jake thinks I'm only attracted to asshole men, and he thought maybe a date with a woman would help me gain some clarity or something."

"Are you serious?"

"It sounds so much worse now that I'm explaining it to you."

"Well, it's pretty terrible," I said. "My sister is gay, and I'd never try to get her to date a man. I mean, come on, what century is it?"

"He's not trying to turn me straight. I think he just figured I needed to get out of my comfort zone. Mix things up. His original idea was worse. He was trying to get me to have sex with a woman. I refused to budge on that."

I gaped at him. "Some friend."

Preston shook his head. "I shouldn't have let him talk me into this. Listen, I'm sorry. When we saw you at the bar, I said you were pretty. I don't have to be straight to appreciate female beauty. He said he'd get your number for me. I didn't think he was serious. But suddenly, there he was, talking to you. I didn't want to be a jerk and not text you after all that."

"But why go out with me at all?" I asked. "You could have texted and said your friend overstepped and you weren't really interested."

"I should have, but I didn't want to hurt your feelings," he said. "And then today at coffee, I was having such a nice time. You're so easy to talk to and I thought hanging out a little more would be fun. I'm sorry I wasn't honest with you."

I took a deep breath and shrugged, letting my arms drop. "Well, I've had worse first dates. Do you still want some shopping help?"

"Really?"

"Sure, why not? But you have to promise me one thing."

"What's that?"

"I get to pick your first casual Friday outfit, and you have to promise to wear it. And text me a selfie."

He narrowed his eyes and crossed his arms. "I don't know."

"Trust me." I grinned.

"Okay, well, I suppose I deserve it." He gestured at the clothes surrounding us. "Do your worst."

"Gay?" Hazel asked, her eyebrow arching behind her glasses. "That definitely presents a compatibility problem."

"I can't believe I didn't realize it at the bar," Nora said. "Normally I can sense these things, even from a distance."

"I feel like I should have known," I said. "Anyway, it was a relief when I found out the truth."

"A relief?"

"Well, yeah," I said. "It explains why I wasn't attracted to him. I was starting to worry I was a cliché—the nice girl who's only attracted to jerks."

"Don't be silly," Nora said. "So, what clothes did you pick out for him?"

"Nothing terrible," I said.

"Why not?" Nora asked. "He lied to you."

"He did, but like I told him, I've had worse first dates. And I think he just needed a change of pace. Granted, asking me out under false pretenses wasn't cool. But I had a lot of sympathy for him. He told me a little more about his breakup and it was pretty bad. Besides, I liked him."

"It's understandable," Hazel said. "Remember Joey Schilling?"

"The guy you dated freshman year?" I asked.

Hazel nodded. "Turns out he was gay. I experienced a

similar sense of relief at realizing the reason for our lack of compatibility. I wasn't angry with him, either."

"See?"

"Okay, feelings, self-discovery, yadda yadda," Nora said, waving her hand around. "What does he have to wear to work on Friday?"

"A Jack Daniels t-shirt, black leather jacket, and a pair of distressed jeans," I said. "Oh, and Converse high tops. I'm telling you, he looked freaking adorable. It didn't even look like him."

"You had the opportunity to make him go to work in a Speedo, and you chose that?" Nora asked.

"I didn't want to be mean," I said. "Just help him get out of his comfort zone a little."

"I approve," Hazel said. "And you're right, gay is not the worst you've encountered on a first date."

I raised my glass. "Indeed."

Nora's lip protruded in a pout. "Fine, you're probably right. I'm just glad he wasn't a serial killer."

I took a sip. "That's one dating disaster I've never encountered."

"Well, don't jinx it," Nora said.

"That doesn't pose a real danger," Hazel said. "There's no such thing as a jinx."

"Maybe, maybe not," Nora said and finished off her glass of wine.

I leaned back into my bean bag chair and ran my fingers through the fuzzy yellow fabric. My date with Preston hadn't been awful, but it had certainly been disappointing. Was it too much to ask to meet a guy who was ready for a relationship, attractive, and straight? It didn't seem like I was asking for the world, here. It wasn't like I was chasing millionaires, or refused to date blond men, or had other criteria that made dating more difficult.

I simply wanted a good man. Someone I could connect with. Share a life with. Someone who did it for me in and out of the bedroom.

Was he out there somewhere? I was really starting to wonder.

EPISODE 4

EVERLY

*T*he bar was crowded, so we'd chosen a table near the back. It was dim back here, but at least we could hear each other.

"What's with the crowd?" Nora asked, glancing around as she perched on the bar stool. "It's a Tuesday."

"Good question," I said. We came to this bar once in a while—the martinis were excellent—but it wasn't usually this busy.

"Taco Tuesday," Hazel said, nodding toward a waitress carrying a taco platter to a nearby table.

"Ah," Nora and I both said in unison. Taco Tuesday explained everything.

A waitress brought our drinks and I stirred my martini with the speared olive.

"Am I mistaken, or did you have a date the other night, Miss Everly?" Nora asked.

I nodded. "Chad."

"The abs guy?" Nora asked. "He was a gym bro, wasn't he?"

"What's a gym bro?" Hazel asked.

"You know, a guy who's really into fitness," Nora said. "Spends most of his free time at the gym, both for working out and socializing. Really into supplements. Not much else going on up here." She tapped her temple.

Unfortunately, that was pretty accurate.

"Kind of," I said. "Although a night of talking about supplements and training regimens would have been better than what actually happened."

"Uh-oh," Nora said. "What went wrong this time?"

CHAD HELD the door for me as we walked into the bar. Noise spilled out into the evening air. I'd never been here before, and I didn't want to judge, but at a glance it didn't look like my usual crowd. It reminded me of a college bar right after finals week. The kind of place that specialized in cheap well drinks and shots. It smelled like the nineties—mostly beer mixed with cucumber melon body spray and Axe deodorant.

People gathered in knots around tables, talking and laughing over their drinks. My black sheath dress and party-pink heels had seemed like perfectly good date attire when I'd chosen them, but here I felt overdressed. The men were dressed casually, most in jeans, and the women were the same.

We wove our way through the crowd and stopped at a small bar-height table.

"I'll go get us drinks," Chad said, raising his voice above the noise.

"Thanks." I had no idea if he could hear me.

I'd been introduced to Chad through a co-worker. We'd texted for a few weeks before I'd decided to take a chance and go out with him. He'd seemed nice enough, although he had sent a lot of pictures of his abs. Granted, the girls and I had stalked him on social media, and peek-a-boo abs pics were a large part of his online persona. Apparently, that was his thing.

He was attractive, in an athletic way. Tall and big, with an imposing physical presence. He was in great shape, with wide shoulders and thick arms. I imagined he'd played sports in high school—maybe college, too.

Not my usual type, necessarily—if I had a type, other than *wrong*—but he'd made me laugh a lot, so that had to count for something. Funny was good. And let's be honest, the abs didn't hurt.

Funny, and nice abs? That was worth a date, in my book.

I glanced over at the bar, wondering how Chad was going to get close enough to order anything. It was packed.

My mouth dropped open as I watched him grab a smaller guy beneath the arms. He lifted him up like a little kid and set him out of the way. Then he moved into his spot at the bar and flagged down the bartender.

Wow. Well, that was something.

A man dressed in a t-shirt with the bar logo came out onto a small stage with a microphone in his hand. "Hey party people!"

The crowd erupted with cheers.

"I'm Maverick, and I'll be your host tonight." He pulled a large box closer to the edge of the stage. "Who's ready to win some prizes?"

More cheering.

Chad came back with two beers. I wondered what it was about me that had made Chad think I was a beer drinker, but I thanked him anyway.

Maverick—I wondered if that was his real name or if he

was a male stripper on the side—held his hands up for quiet. "Okay, first up. Trivia!"

More cheers.

"This place is great, right?" Chad asked. "They have the best trivia nights. I'll win you something good."

People started crowding around the stage, nearly surrounding our table. One guy got a little too close and Chad casually shoved him out of the way, then winked at me.

Maverick started posing pop-culture questions to the crowd. It was clear the game wasn't meant to be challenging. The questions were basic. People shouted out answers—I had no idea how Maverick could tell where the responses came from—and he tossed random bar swag into the crowd.

Chad yelled out his answer each time and scowled when he didn't win. "We're too far back. Let's get closer."

"Oh, I don't think—"

He took my hand and pulled me with him, either ignoring or not hearing my protest. I shuffled along behind, my heels sticking to the floor so badly one of them almost came off.

Gross.

Chad cut a path through the crowd, people moving aside for him like Fezzik in *The Princess Bride*. He held my hand, leading me along, and didn't stop until we were near the stage.

"What actor is known for the phrase *I'll be back*?" Maverick asked.

"Ah-nold!" Chad shouted, in a silly mimicry of an accent.

Everyone else in the place yelled the same thing, and Maverick picked a winner on the other side of the bar.

"Damn," Chad said.

"All right, people, let's take this to the next level,"

Maverick said, and the crowd erupted with renewed cheers. "It's time for the bonus round."

Two bouncer-types—big guys wearing bar t-shirts—started clearing a space in front of the stage, making people move back.

Chad kept us near the front. I had no idea what was going on, but I wasn't so sure I wanted a front-row seat.

"Okay, party people," Maverick said. "I need volunteers for tonight's bonus challenge."

Chad's hand shot into the air and he put his other arm roughly around my shoulders. "We've got this, Mav!"

"You two," Maverick said, pointing at us.

"Yes!" Chad did a fist pump, his arm still around me.

Oh god.

As Maverick picked more couples, Chad nudged me into the center.

"Chad, I don't know about this," I said, trying to be discreet. "What's a bonus challenge?"

"Don't worry, babe, this will be fun."

Babe? Where had that come from? I glanced down at my dress and heels. Maybe bonus challenge meant something simple. After all, the trivia questions had been easy.

Chad lifted his arms overhead in a stretch, then bent his leg and grabbed his ankle to stretch his quad. What was he doing?

"All right, competitors," Maverick said. "Tonight's bonus challenge is balloon busting! The winning couple gets a round of drinks on me."

"Hell yes," Chad said. His eyes were feverish.

Several girls in crop tops and booty shorts came out with blown up balloons.

"Here's how this works," Maverick said. "One of you gets a balloon. The other needs to pop it."

"Easy!" people shouted from the crowd.

"But," Maverick said, holding up a finger, like he was trying to be dramatic. "The balloon will be fastened to one partner's butt." He pointed to his and wiggled his eyebrows. "And the other partner can't touch the balloon with their hands."

Oh no. I did *not* like this.

People laughed and cheered while the booty-short girls went around to each couple.

"Here you go, sweetie," one of the girls said to me. "I'll get it pinned on."

Before I knew what was happening, the petite but big-boobed brunette spun me around—how was she so strong?—and did something to the back of my dress while Chad continued limbering up.

"You're all set," she said with a wink.

I twisted around, trying to look. She'd pinned a bright pink balloon to the back of my dress, right on my ass.

At least it matched my shoes?

"Ready?" Maverick asked. "Remember, no touching the balloon with your hands. That'll get you disqualified. Otherwise, all bets are off. First pair to pop their balloon wins. Go!"

I yelped as Chad grabbed my shoulders and spun me so I was facing away from him. He kept his hands on my shoulders and bumped into me a few times, squishing the balloon between us.

"Plant your feet, sweetheart," Chad said, grabbing my hips. "You're about to get the full power of the Chad."

"Chad, wait!"

With his hands tight on my hips, Chad thrust against the balloon with his groin. I staggered forward a step, but he didn't let go. He rammed himself against me again and I could feel the balloon compress. But it didn't pop.

He picked up the pace, thrusting his hips faster. I jerked forward wildly, my hair flying in my face, my heels slipping on the floor.

"Yeah, baby," Chad grunted. "That's it. Come on."

He drove his groin against me like a jackhammer operated by a crazed monkey. The only thing keeping me from falling flat on my face was his painful grip on my hips. And the balloon still didn't pop.

If this was what sex with Chad would be like, I was going to have to pass.

I had no idea what the other couples were doing, but the crowd was almost deafening. Chad rammed against the balloon over and over to the crowd's chants of "Pop! Pop! Pop!"

The balloon compressed and slipped to the side. Chad's groin collided with my ass and he grunted again.

Was that...? He had to be kidding me. Did he have a hard-on?

I tilted my hips forward to get his stupid dick off my ass. I was just about to wrench his hands off my hips and put an end to this when he thrust forward again.

The balloon burst with a loud *pop* and the crowd went wild. Chad let go so fast I staggered forward into the arms of one of the bouncers. He helped me straighten and I whirled around, ready to lay into Chad.

But he was bent over at the waist, holding his groin, a look of debilitating agony on his face.

What had happened?

I reached around to the back of my dress. The balloon was gone—the pieces had flown off when it popped—but I felt something sharp sticking out of my dress.

The pin.

The booty-shorts girl had used an oversized safety pin to attach the balloon to my dress. It must have come loose while Chad was ramming his groin against me, and poked him in the...

"I've been stabbed," Chad choked out, his words so strained I almost couldn't make them out. His face reddened and he dropped to the ground, still holding his man bits. "My dick!"

NORA LAUGHED SO HARD she had to set down her drink to keep from spilling. "He got dick-stabbed?"

I couldn't help but laugh too. "Yep. The pin stuck him right in the peen."

"The chances of that have to be astronomical," Hazel said.

"That's what I thought," I said.

"Was he okay?" Hazel asked.

I nodded. "He wasn't seriously injured or anything. It did take him about twenty minutes before he could get up, though. The paramedics checked him out and said he'd be fine."

"Paramedics?" Nora asked through her laughter. "Did they really need to call an ambulance?"

"Well, that was his fault." I shrugged. "He kept saying he'd been stabbed. Someone called 911."

Nora dabbed the corners of her eyes. "Oh, Everly. What are we going to do with you?"

I sipped my drink. "I have no idea."

"Okay, so maybe no more gym bros," Nora said. "Or guys

who are still hung up on their ex, or narcissistic dicks, or gay men."

"Definitely not," I said.

"Don't give up, honey," Nora said, patting my hand. "Modern dating is a minefield."

Hazel adjusted her glasses. "I agree."

"Thanks, ladies."

I sipped my martini, glancing around the bar. My mother kept telling me that I'd find the right man when I stopped looking. But how was I supposed to meet him if I didn't put myself out there?

I'd just have to keep myself open to the possibilities.

EPISODE 5

EVERLY

*M*y martini was delicious, and boy did I need it. It had been a long, busy week at work. And it was only Wednesday.

"You look tired," Hazel said. There wasn't any judgment in her observation, just a simple statement of fact.

She wasn't wrong.

"I am tired." I set my martini down. "Work has been crazy. My boss fired two people on Monday, so now everyone's in a panic. And of course they all come to me. I feel like I've become the office therapist."

Nora reached over and squeezed my arm. "That doesn't surprise me. You're good at making people feel better."

"Thanks. It's just tiring."

I wasn't in the mood to talk about work. I loved my job, and things would settle down soon. They always did. But right now, I needed a break.

"Let's talk about something else," I said. "How's work for you two?"

Nora shrugged and brushed her dark hair over her shoulder. "It's fine. The same, really. I'm working on an article about advances in vibrator technology. So that's fun for obvious reasons."

My cheeks warmed a little—I was such a blusher—and I laughed. "Sounds perfect. What about you, Hazel?"

"My funding was approved, so we start recruiting test subjects next week." She adjusted her glasses. "We're studying the effect of emotional intelligence versus cognitive intelligence on various markers for long-term happiness."

"Wow, sounds fascinating," I said.

"I'm assuming since you didn't text us after your date this weekend that it was either boring, or particularly horrible." Nora arched an eyebrow at me. "Or good and you were waiting to tell us in person so we could all squeal with you over the fact that you finally got some."

I took another sip of my drink. "A combination of the first two. And no, I definitely didn't get some."

"That sucks," Nora said. "If you need any new toy recommendations, I can fill you in on my research."

"Thanks, but I'm fine."

Nora shrugged one shoulder. "Suit yourself. But tell us about your date."

"Well, you know how it is—they always start off okay…"

THE BRUNCH BUFFET WAS LOVELY. My date, Jerry, and I sat in a large booth—he'd requested it—sipping mimosas and eating our mini-quiches, bite-sized pancake skewers with fresh strawberries and whipped cream, and other assorted breakfasty finger-foods.

Jerry had carefully arranged the food on his two plates so nothing touched. I'd met him on a dating app and after exchanging a few messages, he'd suggested we meet for brunch. He was cute in a nerdy way, with dark-rimmed glasses and a button-down shirt. He was an engineer at Boeing. I knew from our messages that he had an interest in aviation, but thankfully he hadn't shown up for our date wearing a vest with his collection of airplane pins or insisted on taking me on a six-hour tour of the Museum of Flight. Not that I'd ever dated someone who'd done that.

Okay, yes I had.

"We should get started," Jerry said. He pulled a folder out of his briefcase—I'd been wondering why he'd brought one—and set it on the table next to his brunch.

"Get started?"

He produced a ballpoint pen and clicked the end. "We have a lot to cover."

"We do?"

"Of course. This is a first date," he said, as if that explained everything. He flipped open the folder, revealing a yellow notepad.

"Are you taking notes?"

"Yes." He held his pen poised over the paper. "First question. Education level?"

I blinked at him a few times, my lips parted. Was he serious?

"So, no college then?" His pen dipped closer to the paper.

"No, I have a degree. I'm just not sure why you're—"

"I already know you're currently employed." He jotted something down. "Do you own or rent?"

"I rent, but that's an odd question."

"That's actually a point in your favor. I own my home, so you being a renter is one less potential complication."

"Wait, complication?"

"Have you been to any foreign countries recently? Particularly any with health warnings from the CDC?"

Why did this feel like the weirdest interview ever? "Um, no."

He looked up. "You're sure?"

"Yes, I think I'd know if I'd been to a foreign country recently."

"Unlikely for rare infectious diseases," he muttered as he wrote. His brow furrowed and he flipped through several pages in his notepad.

"Jerry, I'm not sure what this is about."

"I'm sorry." He flipped back to his notes. "I'm usually much more prepared, but I seem to have left my questions at home. This is very unlike me. I'm having to do this from memory."

"What questions?"

"This is the best way I've found to get to know someone and measure potential compatibility," he said. "I'll be honest with you. I'm thirty-six. I'm not interested in casual dating. If I'm going to spend time and effort dating a woman, I need to know up front whether there's the potential for something long-term."

His dating profile had made it clear he was interested in a long-term relationship. It was one of the reasons I'd started talking to him. He seemed mature and settled, which was appealing to me. Maybe this was simply the engineer in him.

"Okay, I suppose that makes some sense. Do I get to ask you questions, too?"

"Absolutely. I think that would be prudent."

I folded my hands in front of me. "All right, then."

"Great. Next question. Are you up to date on your vaccinations?"

I blinked again. "Um, I think so."

"Excellent. Would you describe yourself as more career-oriented or family-oriented?"

"I don't think you have to be one or the other. I have a job that I love, but I still make time for family."

His forehead creased and he pinched his lips together, *hmm*ing to himself before writing something down. "What about other interests and talents? Are you musical?"

"I sang in the choir in high school and I can hit the high note in 'Take On Me' about half the time."

I'd meant it as a bit of a joke to hopefully lighten the mood—although I really could hit the note, especially after a few drinks—but Jerry didn't seem impressed. He just kept jotting things down in his notebook.

"What about your health history? Any hospitalizations, genetic disorders, serious illnesses, surgeries?"

"I'm not really comfortable giving you my medical information." I was trying to be a good sport, but this kept getting weirder.

"Do you happen to know your waist-to-hip ratio?"

I gaped at him. "You're kidding, right?"

"An adequate waist-to-hip ratio can be a good indicator of suitability for childbearing."

"Are you actually asking me if I have good childbearing hips?"

"My family has a history of large babies. I was eleven pounds at birth. It's an issue. You're very pretty, but possibly too slight."

Jerry didn't strike me as a guy who'd been an overly large baby. He was tall, but thin. Almost too thin for my taste, but I was trying not to get too caught up on physical appearances.

"That's still a very weird question."

"Well, then I have a more direct question."

I took a sip of my mimosa. "More direct than what you've been asking?"

"Do you want children?"

Setting my mimosa down, I let out a breath. Direct or not, that was a fair question if he was this concerned about establishing long-term compatibility. Odd for a first date, yes, but I didn't mind answering. "Yes, I do. Someday."

He wrote another note. "Good."

"Is it my turn to ask questions yet?"

"I have quite a few more topics to cover, but sure." He clicked his pen and held it out to me. "Would you like to take notes? I can give you some blank paper."

"No thanks." I hesitated, not sure what I wanted to ask. I just didn't like the feeling that I was being interviewed. "Do you want kids?"

"That's the goal."

"The goal? You make it sound so clinical."

He looked up as footsteps approached our table. "There you are."

There who was?

A middle-aged woman with graying hair wearing a floral blouse and light-wash jeans stopped beside our table. My lips parted in surprise as she slid into the booth next to Jerry.

"How are we doing?" she asked, her voice sugary sweet.

"I'm not finished, so I haven't calculated the percentages yet," Jerry said.

I gestured to the woman. "Um, who is this?"

"Sorry," Jerry said. "This is my mother, Linda."

His mother? Before I could ask why his mother had just sat down with us—and what Jerry meant by percentages— he kept talking.

"Are you allergic to pet dander?"

"Um, no."

He leaned back in his chair. "So far, she checks out. Her medical history might bring up something that I haven't found yet, but she looks healthy."

Linda peered at me. "She does. Good color in her cheeks. How are her hips?"

"She looks a bit small-boned, but we could take some measurements to be sure."

I sputtered as they talked about me like I wasn't there, but I couldn't seem to get a coherent word out.

"We'll do a six-month trial," Jerry said. "I think we should start immediately with a dog, see how we do with co-parenting a pet. Everly, if your rental doesn't allow pets, the dog can sleep at my place, but I'm going to need you to pull your weight as far as pet care and training time."

"What?"

"Jerry, I think you're getting a little ahead of yourself," Linda said.

"Yes, he is. Thank you."

"I haven't seen her eat yet," Linda said.

I blinked at her a few times. "Excuse me?"

"Go ahead." She gestured at my food, indicating I should eat. "Take a bite."

"Why do you want to see me eat?"

"How many drinks has she had?" Linda asked, completely ignoring my question.

Jerry glanced up from his continued note-taking. "Just the one."

"Acceptable, although if this is a habit, it could be a problem."

I pointed at Jerry's mimosa. "He has a drink, too."

"He's a man, dear," Linda said.

"A man who drinks pomegranate mimosas," I said.

"I'm sensing stubbornness," Linda said, pointing to Jerry's notes as if she meant for him to write that down. "That, plus the drinking..."

Jerry adjusted his glasses and looked at me. "True. But nobody's perfect. Everly, how do you feel about the names Edwin and Delilah?"

"For what? The dog?"

His brow furrowed again, and Linda snorted.

"No. We'll name the dog Jasper. They're names for our future children. You'll be expected to provide me with a boy and a girl, preferably in that order."

"There are so many things wrong with that, I don't even know where to start."

"I fail to see the problem," Jerry said. "You already told me you want children."

"Yes, someday, with the right man, under the right circumstances," I said. "You do realize a woman can't choose the gender of her baby, right?"

"There are ways to increase the odds of having a baby of the desired gender," Jerry said. "It's all about proper timing and position during intercourse."

"It works, dear," Linda said. "I didn't bring the book, but I'll make sure you get a copy."

This had gone from odd to shockingly bizarre so fast I felt like I had whiplash. How had I gotten myself into this? He'd seemed perfectly normal when we'd exchanged messages. A little stiff, perhaps, but not insane. I felt like I'd entered a parallel universe.

"Listen, Jerry, thanks for brunch, but this is all a little intense." I pushed my plate away. "You seem to be looking for someone very specific, and it's not me."

"On the contrary, by my calculations, you're close to perfect." He tapped his pen against his notepad. "Should we visit the Humane Society today, or is another day better for you?"

"We're not adopting a dog."

Linda put a hand to her chest. "Didn't you ask if she likes pets?"

Jerry flipped through his notes. "I might have missed it. I left my questionnaire at home. I know she's not allergic…"

"I like pets fine; that's not the point," I said.

"Then is Wednesday good for you?" he asked. "I can probably squeeze you in during my lunch break, but you'll need to meet me. I won't have time to pick you up."

"Remember, I volunteer at the library on Wednesdays," Linda said. "That doesn't work for me unless it's before one."

Jerry pulled out his phone. "Let me check my calendar, then. Everly, what's your schedule like this week?"

I stood, quickly grabbing my purse. These people were crazy, and they clearly weren't listening to a word I said. "I'm completely booked all week and also forever. I'd say it was nice to meet you both, but that wouldn't be true. It's been terrifying."

I whipped around and walked away as quickly as my yellow high-heeled sandals would take me. Linda called my name, but I didn't look back.

"WHERE DO YOU FIND THESE WEIRDOS?" Nora asked. "Did his profile say 'psycho seeks long-term basement prisoner'?"

I slumped in my seat. "I don't know. He hid his weirdness very well up until he brought out the notepad and pen. I can still hear the way that stupid pen clicked."

"I can respect his desire for data, but that was over the line," Hazel said.

"He didn't seem to know there *is* a line." I took a sip of my drink. "Maybe I'm meant to be alone."

"Of course you're not," Nora said. "You're just having a streak of bad luck."

"More like I'm cursed."

"Tell you what," Nora said, grabbing my phone. "I'm picking your next date."

"I don't know."

"Think about it," she said, already scrolling through profiles. "We'll trick fate or luck or the universe or whatever's responsible for all these terrible dates you've been having. Plus, I have excellent taste."

"Luck doesn't exist, but there is some merit to her suggestion," Hazel said. "It's possible you're unconsciously sabotaging yourself in your choice of potential partners."

"Why would I be sabotaging myself?"

Hazel adjusted her glasses and shifted in her seat, adopting her *I'm about to give a lecture* posture. "Well—"

"Wait," Nora said, holding up her hand. "This one."

She handed my phone to me, the app open to a photo. He was undeniably attractive. The guy could have been an Instagram model. Dirty blond hair, strong jaw, cute smile. I read his profile. Thirty-one, never married, owned a construction company. He loved sushi, surfing, rock climbing, and his golden retriever, Magnolia.

"He seems..."

"Adorable," Nora said. "Message him."

I held up the phone so Hazel could see. "What do you think?"

She nodded. "I approve."

I took a deep breath. "Okay. I'll message him and see if he responds."

Nora squeezed my arm again. "That's our girl."

EPISODE 6
EVERLY

*M*y phone buzzed as I gave myself a quick once-over in the mirror. I'd chosen a cute yellow dress—my favorite color—with a tapered waist and flared skirt, paired with periwinkle heels I'd borrowed from Nora. A little dressy for a first date, perhaps—especially considering I wasn't sure where we were going, exactly—but it made me feel good, so I decided to stick with it.

Although I'd recently had a string of bad first dates, I was optimistic about today. In an attempt to fool fate, or the universe, or the arbiter of dating luck, Nora had suggested she choose someone for me. She'd found Gunnar Johanessen on a dating app, and so far, he seemed great. We'd messaged back and forth several times. He was charming and funny. Handsome. Owned a construction company.

Today was our first date, and I had a feeling my luck was about to change.

My phone buzzed again, and I picked it up to check.

Nora: *Are you excited for your date?*

Nora: *Do you need help getting ready?*

Me: *Yes, and no, I'm fine. He's picking me up in a few minutes.*

Nora: *What are you guys doing? It's early. Lunch?*

Me: *I think so, but not sure where.*

Nora: *Okay, my love. Have fun!*

Me: *Thanks!*

I checked my lipstick one last time before my phone buzzed again. It was Gunnar, letting me know he was here.

Okay, Everly. Let's go break the bad-luck streak.

He was waiting outside my building. I waved and he got out of his black Ford Explorer to open the door for me.

Nice manners. Good start.

We exchanged hellos and introduced ourselves, since we hadn't yet met in person. He looked exactly like he had in his photos—dark blond hair, blue eyes, muscular build. He wasn't just attractive, he was downright gorgeous.

I resisted the temptation to immediately text Nora and Hazel to gush about how hot he was.

He got in the car and smiled. "You ready?"

"Yep, all set. Where are we going? Lunch?"

He pulled out onto the street. "Oh, right. Yeah, we were going to do lunch—I know a great Thai place—but it turns out I have this wedding to go to."

"A wedding?"

He chuckled. "Yeah. My buddy Diego's getting married today. It's awesome, his fiancée Brittany is a total sweetheart."

Oh god. Was it already happening? Had the bad luck fairy found me already?

"I just have to ask. When we made plans for today, did you not remember the wedding, or...?"

"I did forget. That sounds really bad, doesn't it?" he asked, glancing at me as he merged onto the freeway. "It wasn't on my calendar, and that's totally my fault. I thought it was next weekend. I realized it this morning when my other buddy Tom asked if I'd picked up my tux. I told him I had a date and he said *hey man, just bring her*. So I thought yeah, perfect solution. I get to see my boy Diego get hitched and bring a beautiful date with me."

"Um, tux? Are you in the wedding?"

"Of course. Diego's my man." He jerked his thumb behind him. "It's in the back."

I glanced over my shoulder. There was indeed a black garment bag in the back seat.

"Didn't they have a rehearsal dinner or anything?"

He shrugged. "No, though I wish they would have. I would have remembered this was today."

"Gunnar, I had no idea we were going to a wedding. I would have worn something more appropriate." Which was to say, politely declined and maybe gone out with him for lunch another time.

"First of all, you look incredible. You don't need to change a thing. Second, I'm so sorry. I realize this is totally out of the blue. I'm a spontaneous guy. It keeps life interesting. But sometimes I forget that not everyone can roll with the punches like I do. If you want me to turn around and take you home, it's no problem."

"Well—"

"But before you make your decision," he said, holding up a finger. "My friends are really cool. They've got us wearing monkey suits, but this whole thing is gonna be totally casual. Just, you know, *do you, do you, awesome, kiss her*. Then some good food, lots of wine, a little dancing, some cake. We don't even have to stay very long."

I tucked my hair behind my ear, debating what to do. Going to a wedding on a first date was unconventional at best. But I'd been on some very conventional dates that had turned out awful. Maybe this was part of the universe's way of circumventing my bad luck.

"No, it's fine, you don't have to take me home. I'm sure this will be fun."

He smiled at me again. He really did have a great smile. "Great. Thanks for being so cool about this."

"Wait, I didn't bring a gift. I didn't even get them a card."

"Don't worry about it," he said. "They won't expect anything."

"All right. If you're sure."

"Absolutely sure." Another grin. And the way his arm strained against his shirt wasn't bad either.

This was fine.

I watched as the scenery changed. We drove east out of Seattle, and then kept right on going. Soon we were over the pass, surrounded by trees and mountain peaks. It was beautiful, but I'd assumed the wedding was somewhere nearby, not almost two hours from home.

"Where is this wedding, exactly?"

"It's at a winery out here somewhere." He rooted through the center console, pulling out a crisp white envelope. "The invitation is in there. I think it has the address."

I took the envelope and pulled out the invitation. "Do you even know where you're going?"

"More or less. I'll figure it out."

The invitation did have the address, to Salishan Cellars Winery in Echo Creek.

Ten minutes later—with me as navigator—we pulled into the winery. The grounds were gorgeous. Surrounded by mountains, there were lush gardens and pear trees, the vineyards visible in the distance. It was beautiful.

Gunnar got the garment bag and draped it over his

shoulder, then led me inside the winery. It was beautiful in here, too. Very classy with dark wood beams and soft lighting.

A pregnant woman with dark hair came down the wide staircase. She was dressed in a blouse and slacks, and carried a clipboard. It looked like she worked here.

"Gunnar?" she asked.

"That's me. How did you know?"

She pointed to his garment bag. "That's a tux, and Gunnar is the only groomsman I haven't met." She held out her hand. "Zoe Miles. I'm the events manager. You need to get changed. I can show you where to go."

"Thanks." He turned to me and lowered his voice. "Listen, Everly, thank you so much for being so great. I'm totally going to make it up to you. Just hang in there and I promise we'll have fun later."

Zoe smiled at me. "If you'd like to wait in the tasting room, you're more than welcome."

"Thank you."

Gunnar left with Zoe and I went down the hall to the tasting room. There was still an hour before the wedding started, so I ordered a glass of wine.

The wine was amazing, but I fidgeted in my seat, feeling out of place. Was this more bad first-date luck? Or was it about to turn into the best first date ever? Weddings were lovely, and very romantic. And if Gunnar's friends were as fun as he'd said they were, maybe I'd meet some cool people.

This still had potential. I wasn't going to throw in the towel just yet.

I also hadn't driven myself, so I was stuck until Gunnar decided to leave. But I wasn't letting myself think too hard about that.

Eventually, I joined the crowd of wedding guests in the garden outside. I sat by myself, trying not to look like I was at a total stranger's wedding. At least no one asked me who I was or why I was here.

Gunnar had been right about the wedding being casual. And short. I'd never been to such a quick ceremony. The bridesmaids, dressed in matching peach dresses, came down the aisle, each on the arm of a groomsman. Gunnar winked at me as he passed. He did look great in that tux.

The groom stood at the front, beaming like he'd never been happier in his life while the bride walked down the aisle. Her dress was a simple white gown that looked lovely on her.

From the time the bride reached the front to the end of the ceremony couldn't have been more than ten minutes. It was over before I had a chance to get teary over the vows.

The wedding party exited to the applause of their guests, then Gunnar came back to meet me.

"That was nice," I said.

"Yeah, it was great. Diego's a good guy. I'm happy for him."

I took a deep breath. I wasn't under—or over—dressed. Gunnar had probably been right about my lack of gift going unnoticed. We were in a beautiful winery. This was nice, all things considered. No bad luck in sight.

Or so I thought, until the reception.

Two hours after the ceremony, I stood to the side while Gunnar, the groom, and the other groomsmen—his buddies, as he kept calling them—did yet another round of tequila shots. I wasn't sure who'd brought the tequila, but as soon as the music had started, they'd started drinking —hard.

The bride and her bridesmaids, along with most of the

other guests, were busy dancing. Although *dancing* might not have been the right word. The bridesmaids had been doing shots along with the men, and they were one step away from stripping. Skirts were hiked up, panties showing, and there was so much twerking going in, I felt like we were at a cheesy meat-market club downtown.

Gunnar came over and draped an arm around my shoulder. "Why aren't you dancing with the girls?"

I wrinkled my nose and worked my way out from under his arm. He was starting to sweat tequila. "That's okay, I'd rather not."

"Come on, Everly." His speech was surprisingly clear, considering how much he'd had to drink. "Let's have fun."

He took my hands and I reluctantly let him lead me to the dance floor. The other guys followed, fist-pumping into the air and hollering. The bride backed up into the groom, shaking her ass to the music. He grabbed her hips and started thrusting against her while his buddies cheered.

Gunnar spun me around as the song changed. I stepped backward and ran into a solid wall of person. It was another groomsman. I looked up at his grin and suddenly found myself in between him and Gunnar, while they both tried to grind on me at the same time.

I planted a hand on each of their chests and pushed them away. They laughed and kept dancing, trying to get closer again. More people crowded the small dance floor and the next thing I knew, I was surrounded. The smell of tequila was everywhere, like they'd all been using it as cologne.

A bridesmaid grabbed me and for a second I thought I'd just been saved from the chaos. But she draped an arm around my shoulders, bent her knees, and writhed her way down, almost to the floor. She came up again, sliding her boobs against me, while I stood stiff with shock.

This was worse than a cheap club in a college town on the last night of finals.

Ducking out of the drunk bridesmaid's grasp, I bumped into an older man. He lifted his arms and thrust his groin, over and over, leering at me like he expected me to either jump on him and wrap my legs around his waist, or turn around and bend over so he could jackhammer into my ass.

Which, to be fair, was what half the other guests were doing.

"Cake!"

I had no idea who shouted it the first time, but in seconds, the dance floor erupted in a chant.

"Cake! Cake! Cake! Cake!"

Fists rose in the air, and as if the crowd was a single organism, the writhing, dancing wedding guests moved toward the cake table. The bride and groom stumbled, laughing and pawing at each other, around to the other side of the table. A winery employee was on hand with a knife—and I was about to jump in the way, sacrificing my body to make sure those two crazy drunk people did not get their hands on a sharp implement—when the groom dug his fist right into the cake and shoved a handful in the bride's face.

There was a pause, a shocking moment of quiet when the entirety of the wedding reception took a collective breath. I watched in horror as the bride wiped frosting out of her eyes and flicked it from her hand onto the floor.

She raised her arms above her head and cheered, then took a fistful of cake and smashed it against the groom's groin.

Their guests erupted with cheers. A groomsman dove for the cake, but Gunnar got there first. He raked his hand through the white confection and tossed his handful at the other guy.

I ducked, covering my head as everyone made for the cake.

Staying low, I scurried for the door. People shrieked behind me as cake flew everywhere. Gunnar and his gang of overgrown frat boys led the fray, tossing chunks of white cake and vanilla buttercream.

Somehow I made it out to the lobby with only a single smear of frosting on my dress. I found a bathroom and wiped it clean. By the time I came out, the noise in the reception room had died down. But I didn't go back.

I went out the front doors and stood on the wide porch, breathing in the fresh clean air. The sun had gone down behind the mountains, and the last light of dusk painted the sky pink.

My phone buzzed in my purse, so I pulled it out, my heart sinking as I saw the number. It wasn't Nora, calling to check up on me. After all, my lunch date should have ended already. It wasn't Hazel, either.

It was my boss. Why was he calling me on a Saturday?

"Hi, Mr. Calloway."

"Did we get the new contract from Veta Tech?"

His sharp voice was oddly soothing. The wedding had left me feeling like I was on another planet. At least the crisp monotone of Shepherd Calloway's brusque question was familiar.

"No, we didn't."

"Set a reminder for me to follow up on Monday."

"Sure thing," I said.

He hung up without saying goodbye.

"Okay, then," I said to myself and put away my phone.

"There you are, gorgeous." Gunnar stumbled out onto

the porch, his arm wrapped around one of the brides-maids. He had cake smeared in his hair. "I was looking for you."

I put my hands on my hips, gaping at him. "What are you doing?"

The bridesmaid nuzzled her nose against his neck and traced a finger down his chest. He kept his arm tight around her waist.

"Holy shit, this is the best wedding I've ever been to," he said. "Diego is the fucking man. Let's go."

"What?"

"There's a hotel next door. We're gonna get freaky as fuck." He glanced at the bridesmaid practically dry-humping his leg. "Oh, this is Dee. She's hot, right? Don't even worry about it, Everly, I've got more than enough for both of you."

I blinked at him, my mouth hanging open.

"Or maybe I'll just watch you two," he said, his words slurring. "Dee, you wanna have some fun with my date?"

Dee turned her drunken gaze on me. "Sure. But if I eat her pussy, she eats mine."

"Oh my god," I said. "No. What the fuck, Gunnar?"

"No?" he asked, swaying on his feet. "I thought you'd be down for this. We're just having fun. Don't you like fun?"

"Not that kind of fun." I took a step back, half-afraid they were going to try to drag me bodily to the hotel next door. "You should go. And don't call me. Ever. In fact, I'm blocking your number now because you're probably too drunk and you won't remember."

I held up my phone and took a picture: Gunnar with cake all over him, a drunk as hell bridesmaid hanging on him like a horny monkey. I sent him the picture as evidence, then promptly blocked his number.

"Fine." He and Dee staggered toward the stairs. "You were a shitty date anyway."

I gaped at them as they walked away, ready to call the police if he got in his car. Thankfully, they stumbled toward the hotel next door. I was simultaneously grateful and extremely grossed out.

"Excuse me, Miss, are you okay?"

I jumped at the voice. A man stood at the bottom of the porch steps, as if he'd come from the opposite direction. The first thing I noticed was his wedding ring. The second thing I noticed was that he was drop-dead gorgeous.

But, wedding ring.

"Yes," I said, but even I couldn't fake it now. "No, I'm horrible. My date got wasted and left with a bridesmaid after I said no to a threesome. I didn't even know he was bringing me to a wedding until we were on the freeway. And he said he'd turn around, but I thought it might be fine, even though this was our first date and that's so weird. But Nora picked him and that was supposed to break my bad first-date luck."

I stopped to breathe, knowing I hadn't made any sense.

He walked up the steps, his expression interested rather than baffled. "So, let me see if I have this straight. Nora is your friend, I'm guessing your bestie?"

"Yes."

"And she picked a guy for you to go out with because you've been having bad luck with men. So when that turd-burger over there," he said, pointing in the direction Gunner had gone, "said he was taking you to a wedding on your first date, you went along with it because you figured Nora had your back, so why not be open to the possibilities?"

"Yes, that's exactly it."

"Sweetheart, that sucks. You're super pretty and you

seem really nice. I know we just met, but I have good instincts about these things. You're definitely nice. Maybe even too nice, you feel me? So you were trying really hard to make the best of things today because you couldn't believe this date, of all first dates, would actually go so horribly wrong. This was Nora's guy."

"Yeah, but how do you know all that?"

He grinned and damn it, he really was cute. "What can I say, I'm good. I'm Cooper Miles, by the way."

I shook his hand. "Nice to meet you. I'm Everly Dalton."

"Everly, regardless of the shit you've been through, I think we can call today a win. I'm going to, because I'm really glad I met you. Don't get me wrong, I'm not hitting on you. I said you were pretty, and I wasn't lying. You're very pretty. But I'm totally married and I love my girl like crazy. We're having twins."

"That's so great," I said. "Congratulations."

"It is great," he said, his eyes widening. "Thank you."

Despite everything I'd just been through, I found myself laughing. "Well, thanks, Cooper. I actually feel better."

He pointed at me. "Awesome. That's my job. I mean, not literally. I'm the head grower here, so my job is actually growing grapes. But making people happy is kind of like my second job. An unofficial one, you might say. Although it could totally be official, because I'm really good at it."

This guy was crazy, but at least he was making me laugh. "Yes, you are."

"Hey, listen." His demeanor changed, a seriousness crossing his features. "Do you know how you're getting home?"

My shoulders slumped. "No. The—what did you call him?"

"Turdburger?"

"Yeah, the turdburger drove. And I live all the way in Seattle." I shook my head. "This was a really stupid thing to do. I shouldn't have come."

"Don't worry, Evie—can I call you Evie?—we've got your back." He pulled his phone out of his pocket and tapped the screen a few times, then put it to his ear. "Hi, Cookie, how're you feeling? Awesome. Are you still over at Mom's? Can you ask her if anyone's in the Blackberry cottage tonight?"

A woman's voice answered, but I couldn't hear what she was saying.

"Cool. My new friend Everly was at a wedding over here and her turdburger of a date ditched her. She lives in Seattle and doesn't have a ride home. I'm thinking she can stay here tonight if she wants. Then we can figure out how to get her home tomorrow."

"Oh, Cooper, you don't have to—"

He held a hand up. "I love the shit out of you, do you know that? That's such a good idea. Okay, I'll tell her. Yeah, that would be great. Thanks, Cookie. I love you."

"I can really just call someone to come get me."

"As an alternative," he said, pocketing his phone, "we have a couple of guest cottages here on the property. They're empty tonight, and you're more than welcome to stay."

"Wow, that's so nice of you."

"Our cottages are super comfortable, and have big bathtubs. Amelia suggested we hook you up with an awesome Salishan t-shirt, since you probably don't have pajamas or anything, so you can be comfy. And, you know, we're a winery, so we have lots of wine. Anyway, Amelia's sending Brynn to walk you down there. Brynn's my sister. Amelia would come, but she's really pregnant and it's twins, so she has to lie down a lot. I'd take you myself, but I need to help my brothers deal with the frat party of a wedding you were just at."

"How did you know the wedding turned into a frat party?"

"Zoe texted. She's way too pregnant to deal with those fuckers. My brothers are on their way, although I bet Leo is already there. He probably went through the back. Maybe Chase, too, I don't know. Sounds like it got cray-cray in there, though."

"You have no idea."

"It's okay, we'll deal with it. As long as no one set anything on fire, it'll be fine. As far as tomorrow, we can definitely get you home. Or you can call someone to come get you. It's up to you. But either way, you might as well just relax tonight."

I still felt a little bewildered. Cooper talked really fast. I considered calling Nora and making her drive out here, right this second, to get me. But it was late, and I was already so exhausted. It would be two hours before she could get here, and two hours home.

Plus, a bath sounded magnificent.

"You know what, I'm going to take you up on that. After the day I've had, I could use a relaxing evening."

"I thought so," Cooper said. "Just hang out here, my sister will be right over."

"Thank you so much, Cooper. I really appreciate this."

He smiled. "Anytime. And listen, can I give you a little advice?"

"Um, sure."

"Don't let your bestie pick any more dates for you."

I laughed. "No, I definitely won't."

He tilted his head, narrowing his eyes. "Will you promise me something?"

"I don't know, maybe. Promise what?"

"Don't settle," he said. "Every woman deserves a man who loves her like crazy. Who can't imagine his life without her. That guy's out there, trust me. Wait for him, okay? Don't settle for anything less than a man who loves the fuck out of you. Promise?"

I certainly couldn't argue with that. "Okay, yes, I promise."

"Awesome. Have a good night, Everly. It was great meeting you."

"Thanks. It was great meeting you, too."

Cooper went inside and I waited on the porch for his sister, wondering what Nora and Hazel were going to say when I told them about this disaster of a date.

WONDERING what's next for Everly Dalton? Will she ever find her happily ever after... or even go on a decent date?

FIND out in **Faking Ms. Right**, a hot stand-alone romcom!

KEEP READING FOR A PREVIEW...

FAKING MS. RIGHT: CHAPTER 1
EVERLY

*C*all me weird, but I didn't hate Monday mornings.

Every Monday was a fresh start. A chance to shake off the previous week—or in my case, the disastrous events of the weekend—and move forward.

I didn't want to think about how many Mondays over the last several months I'd felt the need to put a bad first date behind me. But now wasn't the time to ponder my terrible dating luck—even though it was pretty horrific. I'd dish to my girlfriends about it tonight. Over martinis, of course.

For now, I had work to do. And here, in this office, I wasn't Everly Dalton, serial dating disaster. I was Everly Dalton, executive assistant. And I was damn good at my job.

"Good morning, Everly."

I smiled at Nina, the front receptionist. "Good morning. I love your hair today."

Her smile brightened. "Thank you."

I walked down the hallway, smiling and greeting my coworkers. They all said hi and smiled in return. Even Leslie —who hated mornings more than anyone I knew—cracked a little grin over her coffee.

"Morning, sunshine," Steve said. He was dressed in his usual plaid button-down shirt and brown cardigan. He wasn't that much older than me—maybe five or six years—but his clothes made him look like a grandpa from the fifties. I was pretty sure that after work he changed into another cardigan that had a zipper, and probably brown slippers. But he was super nice.

"Morning, Steve," I said. He liked to think he'd nicknamed me sunshine, but he was probably the tenth person to do so over the course of my life. Maybe it was because I wore so much yellow—my favorite color—or because I smiled a lot. His desk was near mine, just across the aisle, so we chatted pretty often. "How's Millie?"

"I think I need to modify her diet again. I might eliminate fish to see if it helps improve her mood."

Millie was Steve's cat, and he was forever tweaking her diet, hoping it would make her be less of an asshole. I'd never had the heart to tell him that Millie was just an old cranky cat, and no special diet would ever make her nice. But it would have crushed him to hear that his cat hated him and probably wanted to murder his face.

"Sounds like a good plan. Keep me posted."

"I sure will," he said and went back to his desk.

Did I really want to hear all about Millie's diet? Not particularly. But it made Steve happy to have someone who listened, so I endured a little bit of cat conversation now and then. I figured if more people made an effort to be friendly, the world would be a much better place.

The truth was, I liked making people happy. It was my catnip. Getting someone grouchy to smile? Best high ever. Like Leslie, Miss I-Hate-Mornings. She'd been resistant to my drive-by good mornings for a while. But eventually I'd worn her down. Stopping by with breakfast muffins and strong espresso a few times had done the trick.

Everyone had a chink in their armor—a place I could get in to find their happy side. Even the grumpiest people were no match for Everly Dalton's sunshine.

Except one man.

Like a cloud passing in front of the sun, casting a dark shadow, a chill spread across the office. I glanced at the time. Eight twenty-seven. Right on time.

His entrance onto the floor created a ripple, like tossing a rock into still water. It radiated out ahead of him, warning everyone of his arrival. The only person I'd ever met who was impervious to my happy-making. My boss, Shepherd Calloway.

Steve looked up at me and winced. I pretended not to notice. I knew he felt sorry for me. Working for Mr. Calloway was not easy. He was cold, harsh, and demanding. He never said thank you, or gave any sort of praise. I'd lived in terror for the first few months I'd worked for him, positive he was going to fire me. He always seemed so angry.

But after a while, I realized that was just the way he was. He wasn't angry at me. In fact, he barely noticed me. Sometimes I wondered whether he'd recognize me if he had to pick me out of a police lineup. He so rarely looked directly at my face that I wouldn't have been surprised to learn he didn't really know what I looked like.

I was pretty sure he knew my name, although he never called me Everly. He never called me anything, really. Just said what he needed to say, without addressing me first. No greetings. No goodbyes. Just, what's on my calendar today? Or, send me the files before my meeting.

The ripple strengthened and I heard his footsteps over

the sudden hushed silence on our floor. I stood, grabbed a stack of paperwork and his coffee—black, just like his heart —and waited.

He didn't look at anyone as he walked down the hall toward his office. No side glances or nods at his employees. Just his steady gait—a man in a perfectly-tailored suit striding toward his office. His dark hair perfectly styled, his stubble perfectly trimmed.

Without so much as a glance in my direction, he walked past my desk. I fell in step behind him as the clock ticked over to eight twenty-eight.

I followed him into his office and set his coffee on his desk, six inches from the edge and slightly off-center, where he wouldn't knock it over when he took off his jacket or bump it when he set down his laptop. I picked up a remote and opened the blinds, stopping them before they let in too much light. He took off his suit jacket, and I was there to take it and hang it on the coat tree near the door.

"Good morning, Mr. Calloway," I said, my voice bright.

He didn't answer. He never did. Not once had he said good morning in return. But I still did it. Every single day. It was part of our routine, so it would have felt weird not to say it.

He sat and opened his laptop. Grabbed his coffee without looking for it and took a sip.

"Did the lawyer from Duggan and Nolan send over what I asked for?" His voice was smooth and even, without a hint of emotion. Everything he said was delivered in that same tone. People were terrified of Shepherd Calloway, but it wasn't because he yelled. He didn't get loud and berate people when they made mistakes. He froze them. His ice-blue eyes and low voice were more chilling than any tirade could have been. He was a man who could make your heart stop with a glare.

"Yep, no issues there." I placed a thick manila envelope on the side of his desk.

He touched it with two fingers and shifted it up about an inch.

"I also have something for you from Mark in Accounting." I set a file folder directly on top of the envelope, making sure the edges lined up nicely.

"Why didn't he give it to me himself?" he asked.

Because everyone is afraid of you, so they come to my desk early and pretend they didn't realize you wouldn't be in your office yet. "I suppose because you weren't in."

He didn't respond.

"You have meetings at ten, noon, and three." I quickly flipped through his calendar—synced with mine—on my phone. "The noon is at McCormick and Schmick's, and I already ordered for you. I moved your dentist appointment to next week because it was going to be too close to your three o'clock. I didn't want you to have to rush. But check with me first before you schedule anything for next Tuesday afternoon, because we shouldn't put that off again. Oral health is important."

I paused, although I knew he wouldn't reply. And he didn't.

"I spoke with Leslie about those reports you needed, and she'll have them for you this afternoon. The painting you bought at the Hope Gala last weekend is being delivered to your place later today, so I'll run over there and sign for it. That means I'll be out of the office for an hour or so."

"I need dinner reservations for tomorrow," he said, still not looking up. "For two. Tulio or Assiaggo are acceptable.

Not Canlis. And book a room on Maui for ten days, beginning Saturday. One of the usual resorts. Doesn't matter which one."

I probably could have indulged in the smug smile I tried to hide. It wasn't like he was looking at me. But I nibbled my lip to stop myself anyway. Dinner for two at Tulio or Assiaggo, but not Canlis, and a last-minute trip to Maui meant he was breaking up with his latest gold-digger, Svetlana.

"Should I clear your calendar?" I asked, knowing he was going to tell me he wasn't going. He'd send Svetlana on the trip to appease her for breaking up. But I had to pretend I didn't know that, and ask anyway.

"No, I'm not going."

"Okay." I indulged in the smug smile. I hated Svetlana. She was a ridiculously gorgeous Bulgarian model—tall, slender, big boobs. A woman that heartless should never have been granted such phenomenal beauty. But the fact that she was stunning wasn't why I hated her. I loathed her because I knew she was only with Mr. Calloway for his money.

She didn't even try to hide it. Strutted around here like she owned half the company—which you could tell she thought was a forgone conclusion. As if he'd marry her. Ugh. The very thought made my skin crawl.

Granted, she wasn't the first gold-digger he'd dated. He attracted them like a super-powered electromagnet. Most of the women he dated were similar: insanely beautiful, of varying intelligence, and primarily interested in the extravagant lifestyle they assumed dating—and even marrying— Shepherd Calloway would give them.

They were in for a rude awakening when they found out Mr. Calloway was not the type of billionaire businessman who lavished his girlfriends with luxurious gifts. Nice dinners, perhaps. And they could attend exclusive events among Seattle's elite perched on his arm. He was certainly a means to being seen.

But from what I could tell, he was just as cold and unemotional with his girlfriends as he was with his employees. And he never spent a lot of money on them. They undoubtedly went into it picturing limo rides to romantic dinners, beautiful jewelry, and fancy vacations. What they got was a man who ignored them almost as much as he ignored me, and who didn't buy them presents—probably because it never occurred to him to bother.

Svetlana hadn't lasted long, but that wasn't a surprise. He'd been seeing her for a couple of months—not that I kept track, really—and it seemed she'd already chafed his nerves more times than he was willing to live with, regardless of what she looked like. And boy, was I glad.

I had no reason to care. Mr. Calloway and I weren't friends. So it shouldn't have mattered to me whether some woman was trying to latch onto him for his money. But it did. I did care about him, even though I knew better. I couldn't help it. I figured I was just built that way and tried to ignore it.

Except for moments like this, when I could privately gloat.

"That's it," he said.

"Sounds good, Mr. Calloway. I'll be at my desk if you need anything."

I said that to him every day, too. And he never replied. But it had become part of our routine, so I said it anyway.

Back at my desk, Steve gave me a reassuring smile. "You sure are tougher than you look."

I shrugged and grinned, feeling a little glow of satisfaction. I always felt that way when people commented on my job. I'd lasted longer than any other assistant Shepherd Calloway had ever had. And I wore that distinction with a great deal of pride.

Only two types of people lasted at this company: people who were close enough to being his peers that they weren't intimidated by him, and people who didn't have to interact with him.

Anyone else usually lasted six months—maybe a year if they were tougher than average.

I'd worked for him for three years—a company record. Before me, he'd gone through assistants like some women went through purses. In one season, out the next. But me? Miss Everly Dalton? I was the only assistant he'd ever had who could actually handle him.

Really, I kind of got off on it. I liked having access to the man everyone was afraid of. The man with the power in this place. I liked the respect my position earned me. Outside these walls, people took me for a sugary-sweet, plain as vanilla, boring blond girl with a big smile.

But my coworkers saw me as something else entirely. They looked at me in awe, wondering how I could possibly handle the big bad wolf. How I never got bit.

It wasn't as hard as they all thought. Once I got to know him—as well as I could, considering he didn't speak to me very much—it was easy to get along with him. Learn his routine. Make sure anything within my control was executed on time. Stay out of his way.

And it worked. I didn't rock the boat. I didn't expect anything I knew he wouldn't give. He wasn't going to be friendly. No asking about my day or thanking me for a job well done. Which was fine. I knew I did my job well, and my pay reflected that.

The situation worked for me, and whether or not he'd ever acknowledge it, I knew it worked for Mr. Calloway too.

I winked at Steve, and grabbed my phone. I had work to do.

~

FAKING **Ms. Right is available at Amazon.com**

ALSO BY CLAIRE KINGSLEY

For a full and up-to-date listing of Claire Kingsley books visit www.clairekingsleybooks.com/books/

For comprehensive reading order, visit www. clairekingsleybooks.com/reading-order/

The Haven Brothers

Small-town romantic suspense with CK's signature endearing characters and heartwarming happily ever afters. Can be read as stand-alones.

Obsession Falls (Josiah and Audrey)

Storms and Secrets (Zachary and Marigold)

The rest of the Haven brothers will be getting their own happily ever afters!

How the Grump Saved Christmas (Elias and Isabelle)

A stand-alone, small-town Christmas romance.

The Bailey Brothers

Steamy, small-town family series with a dash of suspense. Five unruly brothers. Epic pranks. A quirky, feuding town. Big HEAs. Best read in order.

Protecting You (Asher and Grace part 1)

Fighting for Us (Asher and Grace part 2)

Unraveling Him (Evan and Fiona)

Rushing In (Gavin and Skylar)

Chasing Her Fire (Logan and Cara)

Rewriting the Stars (Levi and Annika)

The Miles Family

Sexy, sweet, funny, and heartfelt family series with a dash of suspense. Messy family. Epic bromance. Super romantic. Best read in order.

Broken Miles (Roland and Zoe)

Forbidden Miles (Brynn and Chase)

Reckless Miles (Cooper and Amelia)

Hidden Miles (Leo and Hannah)

Gaining Miles: A Miles Family Novella (Ben and Shannon)

Dirty Martini Running Club

Sexy, fun, feel-good romantic comedies with huge... hearts. Can be read as stand-alones.

Everly Dalton's Dating Disasters (Prequel with Everly, Hazel, and Nora)

Faking Ms. Right (Everly and Shepherd)

Falling for My Enemy (Hazel and Corban)

Marrying Mr. Wrong (Sophie and Cox)

Flirting with Forever (Nora and Dex)

Bluewater Billionaires

Hot romantic comedies. Lady billionaire BFFs and the badass heroes who love them. Can be read as stand-alones.

The Mogul and the Muscle (Cameron and Jude)

The Price of Scandal, Wild Open Hearts, and Crazy for Loving You

More Bluewater Billionaire shared-world romantic comedies by Lucy Score, Kathryn Nolan, and Pippa Grant

Bootleg Springs

by Claire Kingsley and Lucy Score

Hot and hilarious small-town romcom series with a dash of mystery and suspense. Best read in order.

Whiskey Chaser (Scarlett and Devlin)

Sidecar Crush (Jameson and Leah Mae)

Moonshine Kiss (Bowie and Cassidy)

Bourbon Bliss (June and George)

Gin Fling (Jonah and Shelby)

Highball Rush (Gibson and I can't tell you)

Book Boyfriends

Hot romcoms that will make you laugh and make you swoon. Can be read as stand-alones.

Book Boyfriend (Alex and Mia)

Cocky Roommate (Weston and Kendra)

Hot Single Dad (Caleb and Linnea)

~

Finding Ivy (William and Ivy)

A unique contemporary romance with a hint of mystery. Stand-alone.

~

His Heart (Sebastian and Brooke)

A poignant and emotionally intense story about grief, loss, and the transcendent power of love. Stand-alone.

~

The Always Series

Smoking hot, dirty talking bad boys with some angsty intensity. Can be read as stand-alones.

Always Have (Braxton and Kylie)

Always Will (Selene and Ronan)

Always Ever After (Braxton and Kylie)

~

The Jetty Beach Series

Sexy small-town romance series with swoony heroes, romantic HEAs, and lots of big feels. Can be read as stand-alones.

Behind His Eyes (Ryan and Nicole)

One Crazy Week (Melissa and Jackson)

Messy Perfect Love (Cody and Clover)

ABOUT THE AUTHOR

Claire Kingsley is a #1 Amazon bestselling author of sexy, heartfelt contemporary romance and romantic comedies. She writes sassy, quirky heroines, swoony heroes who love their women hard, panty-melting sexytimes, romantic happily ever afters, and all the big feels.

She can't imagine life without coffee, her Kindle, and the sexy heroes who inhabit her imagination. She lives in the inland Pacific Northwest with her three kids.

www.clairekingsleybooks.com